Dedication

To my family, who had more faith in my words than I did.

Without you, Wobblebottom and his farts would still be locked in my bottom drawer.

Contents

CHAPTER 1
A Quest Begins... with Butter

Once upon a ridiculous time, in the mildly majestic Kingdom of Wobblealot, where dragons occasionally delivered the mail and the royal anthem was performed entirely on a Cajon, there lived a king with an enormous crown and even more enormous problems.

His name was King Arthur. And his problem was… his horse.

It was missing.

"Where in the name of Excalibur's itchy hilt is my horse?!" bellowed Arthur, standing in the Royal Stables, wearing only one boot and half a tunic. "We've got a quest today! A real one! With maps and danger and probably at least one riddle!"

The stable boy, a timid creature named Kevin, trembled behind a bale of hay. "Your majesty, your horse ran off with the jousting instructor's daughter. Again."

Arthur sighed the sigh of a man who knew deep in his soul that his horse was in love. Not the romantic kind, of course. No, his horse was in love with the idea of becoming a champion jousting steed. And

ONCE UPON A RIDICULOUS TIME IN THE KINGDOM OF WOBBLEALOT

ONCE UPON A RIDICULOUS TIME IN THE KINGDOM OF WOBBLEALOT

D.R. FOSTER

for reasons only the gods of hay understood, the horse had decided that the jousting instructor's daughter was the fast track to fame and oats.

"Fine," he muttered. "Desperate times call for... unconventional measures."

And so, he turned to the last stall at the end of the stable. The one marked with a sign that read:

DO NOT RIDE. HIPPO. SLIPPERY WHEN EXCITED.

Inside was an extremely large, extremely pink hippopotamus. One eye was covered with what looked suspiciously like the bottom of a jam jar, tied in place with a bit of string. He was chewing on a watermelon rind, as if questioning how many minutes stood between him and lunch.

"Hello, Wobblebottom," Arthur said, patting the hippo's squishy side. "How do you feel about a bit of royal adventuring?"

Wobblebottom blinked slowly.

Then he farted.

Loudly.

The sound echoed through the stone stable like a battle trumpet.

"Good enough for me," said the king.

And so, after an awkward and slippery mounting process involving a ladder, a winch, and a generous amount of butter, King Arthur finally managed to settle himself atop Wobblebottom. With a grunt of triumph, he declared, "You, my friend, are now officially Sir Wobblebottom, Royal Steed of the Realm."

As the pair clomped (well, wobbled) out of the Royal gates of Wobblealot on their first glorious quest, the kingdom, ever accustomed to oddities, fell into a puzzled silence, watching as the king and his hippo steed trudged into the unknown.

"That," said Sir Spatula, flipping an imaginary pancake, "is either the bravest thing I've ever seen... or the dumbest."

"I vote dumbest," muttered Merlin the Unreliable, who had just watched his staff transform into a baguette and was now trying to figure out how to turn it back into a staff.

Arthur squinted one last time at his map, where a mystifying greasy "X" marked the fabled Golden Gravy Boat, hidden somewhere in the deeply inconvenient land of Grizzleham. He tucked it away with the grim resolve of a man who had once gotten lost in his pantry.

With Sir Wobblebottom's flatulence sounding off like a mournful trumpet, they rode forth into the unknown, uncertain, underprepared, but undeniably committed to the dumbest quest the realm had seen since the Great Pudding Rebellion.

CHAPTER 2
RIDDLE ME THIS
(PLEASE, I'M LOST)

The road to Grizzleham was long, winding, and slightly dubious.

King Arthur bounced ungracefully atop Sir Wobblebottom, who moved with all the speed and coordination of jelly in a wheelbarrow. Every step was accompanied by a moist squelch, a regal wobble, and the occasional honk that sounded alarmingly like a tuba in distress.

"So," Arthur said, pulling out the scroll and squinting at it upside-down, "according to this map, we need to pass the Bridge of Reasonable Peril, after that, it's just a quick jog through the Screaming Ferns and left at the Flaming Turnip Stand."

Sir Wobblebottom blinked at him.

"I agree," Arthur said solemnly. "Turnips are the worst."

As the sun climbed lazily into the sky (and then immediately took a nap behind some clouds), the duo finally reached the bridge.

It was... underwhelming.

Made of slightly mouldy wood and some much frayed rope, the Bridge of Reasonable Peril stretched across a bubbling creek that might've once been threatening, but now just looked like it needed a good scrub. It appeared that even the troll had left town.

Standing in front of it was a shrub.

A talking shrub.

With glasses.

"HALT," declared the shrub, in the wheezy voice of someone who once swallowed a pinecone for no good reason and instantly regretted it. "To cross this ancient, sacred bridge, you must answer three riddles! Or maybe two. Honestly, I lost count after lunch."

Arthur leaned forward in his saddle-hippo. "And who, exactly, are you?"

"I," said the shrub, puffing out a leafy chest, "am Gregory the Riddler Shrub, Guardian of the Perilous Pass and certified riddle master. Also, part-time poet and full-time disappointment to my hedge fund parents."

Sir Wobblebottom attempted to eat him.

"NO! NO! NO!" Gregory cried, shaking off a slobbery leaf. "No munching the riddle master! That's cheating."

"Fine," Arthur sighed. "What's the first riddle?" Gregory cleared his throat.

"I speak without a mouth and hear without ears.

I have no body, but I come alive with fear—wait. No. That's wrong. Sorry. That's from my spooky Halloween set. Hold on."

He rustled through a pouch at his base, pulling out a small stack of cards. "Ah, here we go." "Ahem.

What has keys but can't open locks,

Sits on laps but doesn't wear socks?"

Arthur frowned. "Is it... a sockless butler named Gregory?" "No!"

Sir Wobblebottom belched.

"...A piano," Arthur guessed.

Gregory gasped. "How did you—?! No matter. You were probably trained by riddling monks or—whatever. Second riddle!"

He struck a dramatic pose.

"The more you take, the more you leave behind.

Unless you're a kangaroo. Then it's confusing."

"Footsteps," Arthur said without blinking.

Gregory stared at him. "That was... that was supposed to be a tricky one."

"I had a riddle calendar last year," Arthur said smugly. "April was all footsteps."

"Fine!" snapped Gregory. "Final riddle!"

He glared at them both, dramatically tossing the last card over his shoulder.

"What gets wetter the more it dries?"

Sir Wobblebottom raised a giant foot and squashed a mushroom.

Arthur tilted his head. "A towel."

Gregory made a sound like a deflating balloon.

"I hate this job," he mumbled.

"Can we pass now?" Arthur asked.

Gregory sighed, dramatically turning sideways. "FINE. But beware! The path ahead is filled with danger! Doom! Possibly bees! And—wait, wait—do you have snacks?" Sir Wobblebottom sneezed on him.

"...I'll take that as a no," the shrub muttered.

And with a heroic wobble and a tiny trumpet toot (from somewhere, no one was quite sure where), King Arthur and Sir Wobblebottom crossed the Bridge of Reasonable Peril...

...only to immediately fall into a pit labelled "Absolutely Unreasonable Hole: Watch Your Step."

Arthur groaned from the bottom. "I told you the map was upside down."

Sir Wobblebottom just farted.

Chapter 3
Teapots and Treachery

After an embarrassing climb out of the absolutely Unreasonable Hole—featuring three vines, two squirrels, and one very sarcastic mushroom—King Arthur and Sir Wobblebottom found themselves at the edge of a forest.

A very... twinkly forest.

"Welcome to the Enchanted Forest of Whimsywood," King Arthur read aloud from the sign. "Warning: Sparkles may be permanent."

Wobblebottom blinked.

Then sneezed.

Glitter erupted from his nostrils like a sneezy unicorn explosion.

"Well," King Arthur said, brushing sparkle-dust from his royal eyebrow. "At least we'll be easy to spot by any lurking monsters."

The forest itself looked like it had been decorated by a unicorn and a fairy trying to out glitter each other. Trees shimmered with pink leaves. Flowers giggled when stepped on. A passing squirrel wore a tiny top hat and gave Arthur a judgmental nod.

Still, they trudged forward. Or rather, Wobblebottom waddled forward with Arthur clinging to his back like a noble sack of potatoes.

Just as the sunlight dimmed and a gentle breeze played a questionable jazzy tune, Arthur heard a faint clink-clink-clink up ahead.

"Sounds like someone's making tea," Arthur whispered.

They rounded a bend—

And found themselves face-to-face with a platoon of angry, enchanted teapots.

Each one had spindly porcelain arms, twitchy lids for hats, and expressions of deep, steaming rage. They were arranged in tight formation, like a very polite but furious army.

"Halt in the name of Lady Oolong!" squeaked a tiny floral teapot with a chip in its spout.

"This is Whimsywood. Tea time is sacred. You've entered without a reservation!"

Arthur squinted. "I didn't know teapots had an army." The teapot army advanced, clinking menacingly.

"We demand tribute!" cried the chipped commander. "Preferably biscuits, scones, or a mild jam."

"I've got a packet of slightly damp cheese crackers," Arthur offered, pulling a crumbly lump from his satchel.

The teapots gasped in horror.

"Cheese? With tea?! Barbarian!"

Sir Wobblebottom, sensing tension—or perhaps just hungry— snuffled forward and gently nudged one of the teapots with his nose.

Then, in a moment that would be sung about by forest bards for weeks, he opened his mouth...

...and swallowed it whole.

GULP.

Silence.

Arthur blinked. "Oh dear."

"ASSAULT!" cried the remaining teapots. "DEPLOY THE SUGAR CUBES!"

A swarm of tiny, angry sugar cubes flew out from the trees like caffeinated bees, pelting Arthur and Wobblebottom with surprising accuracy.

"Retreat!" Arthur shouted, ducking a cinnamon stick missile.

"To the bushes!"

They galloped (well wobbled) through the glittery underbrush as teapots gave chase, firing tea bags like slingshots and yelling things like "INFUSE THIS!" and "SCONE YOU LATER!"

Finally, after what felt like an hour (but was probably seven minutes and a lot of wheezing), they crashed through a hedge, tripped over a root, and landed in a clearing.

All was quiet.

Arthur peeked up from under Wobblebottom's behind. "I think... we lost them."

Wobblebottom sat heavily on a log, victorious and gassy.

Arthur slumped beside him, covered in glitter, sugar cubes, and what he hoped was jam.

He pulled out the map again. "Well. The good news is, we're still on course to Grizzleham."

He paused.

"...The bad news is, this part of the forest is labelled 'Here Be Slightly Haunted Things.'"

Sir Wobblebottom snored. Then farted.

Arthur sighed.

"Brilliant."

Chapter 4
The Cursed Pants
of Sir Flatulence
Ye OLDe
GHASTLY
PANTS
INN & LAUNDRY SERVICE
Est 21tM
LAST THURSDAY)

Night fell over Whimsywood like a particularly large curtain made of ominous fog and poor decisions.

King Arthur was cold, damp, and still mildly sticky from the sugar cube ambush. Sir Wobblebottom, on the other hand, seemed perfectly content, snoring atop a mossy rock and occasionally releasing sounds that could only be described as musical plumbing disasters.

"I swear," Arthur muttered, brushing leaves from his royal tunic, "if we don't find shelter soon, I'm going to start hallucinating polite sandwiches."

Just then, through the mist, a crooked sign creaked into view:

Ye Olde Ghastly Pants Inn & Laundry Service

(Est. 2:17 PM, Last Thursday)

"An inn!" Arthur declared. "Finally, a break from the madness!"

He knocked on the door. It immediately fell off its hinges with a ghostly wheeeeeze.

Inside, the lobby was dimly lit by flickering chandeliers and one glowing portrait of a cat who looked like it knew your dark secrets. A dusty bell sat on the counter. Arthur gave it a tap.

DING.

A moment later, a translucent figure floated up through the floor. It wore a waistcoat, half-moon glasses, and a name tag that read:

GORDON, SPECTRAL INKEEPER & HAUNTED HOSPITALITY SPECIALIST

"Welcome," Gordon said in a voice like wind through a very dissatisfied tunnel. "We offer single rooms, double rooms, and the Unholy Honeymoon Suite, which comes with complimentary ghosts."

"We'll take… the one furthest from cursed teapots and emotional trauma," Arthur said.

"Room 4B it is," Gordon said, floating them a key made of mist. "Beware the wardrobe. And please do not wear anything you find inside it. Especially not the pants."

Arthur raised an eyebrow. "What happens if someone wears the pants?"

"They dance and they fart," Gordon said solemnly. "And they do not stop"

Arthur frowned. "What do you mean, 'do not stop'?"

"The dancing. And the farting," Gordon added, as if this was common knowledge.

 Room 4B was, absolutely horrifying. The wallpaper was peeling, the bed floated three inches off the floor, and the chandelier appeared to be whispering some form of insults.

Arthur sighed, peeled off his damp clothes, and opened the wardrobe.

Inside was exactly one item: a pair of pants.

They shimmered.

They sparkled.

They... purred?

Arthur frowned. "Surely these can't be the cursed ones. They look my size."

Sir Wobblebottom snorted from the corner.

"I'm just going to try them on for a second," Arthur said, already one leg in.

The moment both legs were inside, the pants shuddered— and suddenly Arthur's limbs began flailing wildly in a complicated series of interpretive dance moves he absolutely did not know. The noises coming from his behind were the most horrific sounds he had ever encountered.

"NOPE. THIS IS A CURSE," he yelled as he jazz-handed into a wall.

Sir Wobblebottom watched with vague interest as Arthur tumbled through the room, disco-stepping and moonwalking uncontrollably. A ghostly trumpet blared from the ceiling. The pants were dancing to the tune of the farts coming from King Arthur, not very kingly at all.

"I can't stop!" Arthur cried, now twerking toward the fireplace. "THEY HAVE A MIND OF THEIR OWN!"

Sir Wobblebottom waddled over, stared for a moment, then casually bit the waistband off the pants.

There was a loud POP, a puff of glitter, and Arthur collapsed into a nearby chair—pant less, dizzy, and emotionally scarred. "Well," he panted, "I'm never trusting wardrobe fashion again."

The pants lay in the corner, twitching ominously.

Just then, Gordon reappeared through the wall.

"Would you like turndown service?" he asked.

Arthur pointed at the pants. "I-I'd l-like ..." he decided it was better not to finish that sentence.

They left the inn the next morning before sunrise. Arthur had borrowed a tablecloth as temporary trousers. Wobblebottom had apparently made friends with the haunted chandelier, which now dangled from his back like misplaced jewellery.

"So far," Arthur muttered, "this quest has involved: glitter, angry porcelain, breakdancing pants, and a symphony of flatulence."

Sir Wobblebottom farted loudly, blissfully unaware that Arthur was even remotely upset.

Chapter 5
Attack of the Squirrel
rumpy
homes
nights
say "MEH"

The morning was unusually crisp and twitchy.

Birds chirped sullenly. The wind whooshed with dramatic flair. Somewhere in the distance, a cow mooed in a way that implied it knew something deeply unsettling.

Arthur tightened the tablecloth-turned-trousers around his waist. "Alright, Wobblebottom," he said, glancing at the increasingly wrinkled map, "we take a left at the Whispering Ferns, go straight past the Grumpy Gnomes' Picnic Area, and then—"

Thunk.

Something hit him in the face.

It was a tiny acorn.

Then another.

Then five more.

"I AM UNDER ATTACK!" Arthur shrieked, flailing wildly.

From the trees above came a cackling voice, high-pitched and theatrical:

"BEHOLD! THE WOODLAND WRATH OF
BARON ACORN VON TWITCHWHISKERS!"

Out of the branches leapt a squirrel.

But not just any squirrel.

The squirrel wore a tiny top hat, red velvet
cape, a golden acorn medallion, and an
expression of pure, unfiltered drama. He
landed with a flourish, flinging his arms wide.

"I have been observing you, travelers," he said,
dramatically pacing atop a mossy log. "You
appear lost, confused, glittery, and
questionably dressed."
Arthur blinked. "You're a talking squirrel."

"I am a noble squirrel," Baron Twitchwhiskers
corrected.

"Former Duke of the Hollowed Log, twice-voted
'Most Likely to Monologue', and current self-
appointed Guardian of These Woods."

"Right. Okay," Arthur said, leaning down to
Wobblebottom. "Do you think I'm dreaming?

Because this feels very dream-like. Or possibly jam-induced." Sir Wobblebottom just licked his nostril.

Baron Twitchwhiskers cleared his throat. "I have heard of your quest. The Golden Gravy Boat of Grizzleham. An object of legend, mystery, and questionable practicality. I, dear sir, shall guide you to it—for I alone know the secret paths!"

Arthur brightened. "You know the way to Grizzleham?"

"Well... no," the squirrel admitted. "But I know a guy who met a bird who once saw it from a hot air badger. Or maybe it was a llama. Details are fuzzy."

Arthur sighed. "So, you're lost."

"I prefer the term navigationally challenged," Twitchwhiskers huffed. "Besides! Who needs accuracy when you have flair?"

He posed again. A passing breeze blew his tiny cape dramatically.

Arthur glanced at Wobblebottom, who was chewing on a flowerpot someone had mysteriously left in the woods. "What do you think? Follow the squirrel?"

Sir Wobblebottom blinked once.

Then sat on the flowerpot.
"Fair enough."

They followed the squirrel through tangled vines, over sticky mushrooms, and across a log shaped exactly like a loaf of bread. Every few steps, Baron Twitchwhiskers would pause, raise one tiny paw, and declare, "Yes, yes... this looks familiar!" before confidently turning in a completely new direction.

After an hour, they were back at the starting point. Arthur stared at the mossy log.

"Is that... is that your acorn throne?"

"Technically, yes," the squirrel admitted, now upside-down and tangled in his own cape.

"But only because the path was so well-designed it looped us back for dramatic effect!"
Arthur flopped onto the grass. "Wobblebottom, remind me: whose idea was it to trust the talking rodent?"

Sir Wobblebottom yawned and accidentally rolled onto the squirrel's top hat.

"I'M FINE," came a muffled voice. "BUT I MAY BE FLAT NOW."

Just then, from beyond the trees, came a new sound: bagpipes. Enchanted bagpipes.

Arthur sat bolt upright. "That's either a marching band or a warning sign."

Baron Twitchwhiskers poked out from under Wobblebottom. "Ah. I forgot to mention the

next part of the forest is guarded by the
Knights Who Say 'MEH'."

Arthur groaned. "Of course it is."

Wobblebottom let out a small squeak of frightened
flatulence.

Chapter 6
THE KNIGHTS
WHO SAY 'MEH.'
We'd rather not.
ROYAL
BYPASS
DESPAIR
DESPAIR
TRIAL-SNACKS
NAP
O'CLOCK

The bagpipes grew louder.

But not majestic-warrior-on-a-battlefield loud.

More like someone was squeezing a very tired goat through a traffic cone while half-heartedly humming.

King Arthur, Sir Wobblebottom, and Baron Twitchwhiskers stood at the edge of a clearing that reeked of old cheese and seem to offer nothing but disappointment.

There, slouched across tree stumps, hammocks, and what looked like a giant beanbag throne, sat a dubious group of knights in rusted armor. Most had their helmets off. One wore bunny slippers. Another was knitting.

Above them, a faded banner drooped between two trees:

THE KNIGHTS WHO SAY "MEH"

"We'd rather not."

A knight with a rusted breastplate and a juice box shuffled forward. "Halt," he said without conviction. "You approach the neutral territory of the Knights Who Say 'Meh'. What do you want?"

Arthur cleared his throat and gave his best noble pose (which wasn't easy in a tablecloth). "I am King Arthur of Wobblealot. We are on a grand quest for the Golden Gravy Boat of Grizzleham!"

The knights blinked at him.

One yawned.

Another muttered, "Do we have to listen to speeches today?"

The first knight sighed. "Yeah, alright. Look. If you want to pass through our territory, you'll need to prove your worthiness." Arthur nodded. "By combat?"

The knight shuddered. "Ugh. No. Too sweaty. You'll need to pass the Trial of Snacks."

From behind the beanbag throne, a small, snacking squire waddled forward holding a tray.

"We present three snack challenges," the head
knight announced, holding up fingers and
counting them out:

1. The Goblet of Lukewarm Root Beer
2. The Very Dry Cracker of Despair
3. The Mystery Cheese of Questionable Origin

Baron Twitchwhiskers immediately fainted.

Sir Wobblebottom leaned in, took one sniff of
the cheese, and gently nudged the tray aside
with his snout, like, "No, thank you, I value
my life."

Arthur stepped forward. "I accept your snacky
trial."

First, he downed the Goblet of Lukewarm
Root Beer in one gulp. It fizzed... and then
burped back.

Next, he bit into the Dry Cracker of Despair.
It crumbled into a million flavorless crumbs,
immediately absorbing all moisture from his
mouth and possibly his soul.

He coughed. "Water... please... or gravy..."

The final test was the Mystery Cheese. It glowed faintly. It hummed. It wobbled slightly when no one touched it.

Arthur looked it dead in its unblinking, dairy eye.

"Wobblebottom," he said solemnly, "if I don't make it, tell Kevin, he's still banned from the stables."

Then—chomp.

Silence.

The forest itself seemed to hold its breath.

Arthur chewed. Once. Twice. Then—swallowed.

He opened his mouth to speak...

...and began glowing slightly.

The knights gasped. One dropped his knitting.

"HE HAS EATEN THE CHEESE AND LIVED," one knight shouted.

Another nodded slowly. "He is... the Chosen One."

A third looked around. "Are we still doing that prophecy bit, or did we cancel it last Thursday?"

The head knight stepped forward. "King Arthur of Wobblealot, you have passed the trial.

You may continue your quest."

Baron Twitchwhiskers peeked out from behind Wobblebottom. "Does that mean there's no more cheese?"

Wobblebottom, without warning, farted loudly.

The breeze carried it over the knights.

Every helmet fogged instantly.

"...We also grant you the Royal Bypass of Eternal Shortcutting," the lead knight said quickly, pinching his nose. "Just go. Please. For the love of all things not cheese-scented."

Arthur bowed. "Thank you, noble knights."

"You're welcome," one said. "Now if you'll excuse us, it's nap o'clock."

King Arthur, Sir Wobblebottom, and Baron Twitchwhiskers journeyed on—glowing, shortcut-granted, and faintly cheese scented.

Arthur checked the map. "Next stop: Grizzleham."

Baron Twitchwhiskers clapped his tiny paws. "Oooooh, I hear they have gravy fountains!"

Sir Wobblebottom wobbled forward with renewed purpose.

He loved fountains.

Especially if they were full of food.

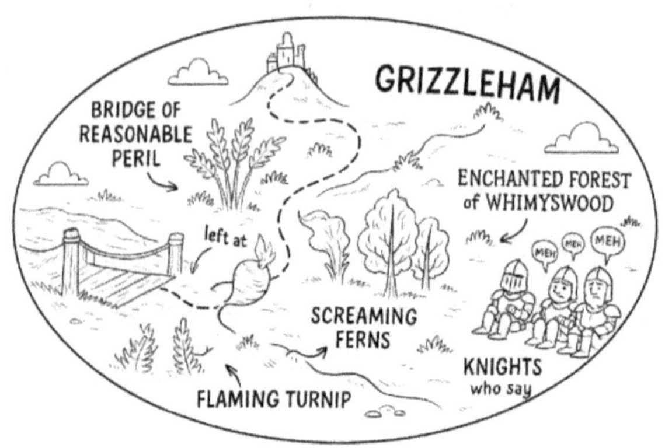

Chapter 7
Grizzleham at Last
(Bring a Towel)

After what felt like approximately 72 snack-

related incidents and 15 unexpected detours, one of which involved an unfortunate misunderstanding with a clan of wandering trolls.

Arthur, Sir Wobblebottom, and Baron Twitchwhiskers finally arrived at the outskirts of Grizzleham.

Grizzleham, as it turned out, was not so much a town as it was a swampy, gravy-drenched kingdom. It sat nestled at the mouth of a very large, very damp river; its mossy buildings huddled together like wet biscuits. Bridges of pancake syrup spanned gravy canals, syrup, and the distinct smell of something potato-y in the air.

Arthur stared at the enormous, bubbling lake of gravy that filled the center of the town square. It glittered like liquid gold under the midday sun— except, of course, for the occasional rogue chunk of something unidentifiable that floated ominously on the

surface, causing locals to avert their eyes and
pretend they hadn't noticed."

"Well..." Arthur muttered, "I did hear Grizzleham
was a little... watery."

Baron Twitchwhiskers adjusted his monocle.
"Water? Oh no, no, no. That's not just water.
That's Legendary Grizzleham Gravy. You
know, the kind that heals wounds, inspires
poetry, and occasionally causes uncontrollable
dance parties."

Wobblebottom, of course, was already wading
through the gravy like it was the most glorious
swamp he'd ever encountered.

"Alright, Wobblebottom," Arthur said, tugging on
his soggy, makeshift trousers. "We need to find the
Golden Gravy Boat. No distractions. Focus."
Baron Twitchwhiskers, however, was already
distracted. "Ooooh, I think I see the royal gravy
fountain. We should pay our respects before
us—"

But before he could finish his sentence, a
very soggy knight in a slightly melted crown
appeared, floating across the gravy on a

paddleboard, holding a scroll in one hand and a ladle in the other.

"Ah, yes. I knew you'd come," the knight said, his voice muffled by gravy bubbles. "You seek the Golden Gravy Boat."

Arthur nodded eagerly. "Yes! We're on a quest for the legendary Gravy Boat that will grant us—"

"Then you must pass the Trial of Gravy," the knight interrupted, raising a scroll. "A test of vision and commitment... via head dunk."

Arthur blinked. "I'm sorry, via a what?"

"To find the Golden Gravy Boat, you must first dunk your head in this bowl of gravy and see what visions it grants you. Only then will the path be revealed."

Arthur frowned. "So, you want me to dunk my head in gravy?"

"Yes," the knight said. "It's tradition."

"But—"

"No but," the knight said, paddling closer. "You want the Golden Gravy Boat, don't you?"

Arthur turned to Baron Twitchwhiskers. "Do I have any other option?"

The squirrel looked thoughtful for a moment. "Well, you could leave. But if you leave, you'll never know if it was the greatest decision of your life. Also, there's a Royal Gravy Parade tomorrow, and I hear they're handing out commemorative spoons."

Arthur sighed. "Alright. Fine. Head dunk it is. But if I come out of this with a gravy beard, we're having words."

With that, Arthur stood at the edge of the Legendary Grizzleham Gravy Lake, his makeshift trousers dripping as he gingerly leaned forward and dunked his head into the warm, gooey depths.

For a moment, there was only darkness. Then— visions.

Arthur saw a giant spoon.

Then he saw a lot of tiny, dancing potatoes wearing crowns.

Then, in the distance, a massive golden boat—surrounded by gravy waves, floating majestically over the lake.

And then, he saw Wobblebottom, wearing an ancient royal crown and doing an elaborate jig with a large, very disgruntled eel.

Then, just as quickly as it had started, everything was gone.

Arthur blinked and pulled his head out of the gravy, coughing and spitting some of the gooey substance from his mouth.

"Did you... Did you see the vision?" asked Baron Twitchwhiskers, wide-eyed.

"I saw a lot of things," Arthur said, dripping with gravy. "But mostly, I think I saw the Golden Gravy Boat. It was on the other side of the lake."

The knight nodded solemnly. "Then you are ready for the final trial."

Arthur sighed. "If it involves more dunking, I may revolt."

The group waded through the lake, approaching a raised platform where the Golden Gravy Boat rested, glinting and glorious. But as Arthur reached out—

The lake trembled.

The gravy frothed, and the air thickened with tension.

A faint whisper, carried on the wind, it sent an icy chill down Arthur's spine.

"I am Lord Lardington. The Golden Gravy Boat is mine."

Arthur froze, his voice barely a whisper. "What was that?"

Baron Twitchwhiskers narrowed his eyes. "What's wrong?"

"Didn't you hear that?" Arthur said, his gaze darting around frantically.

Baron Twitchwhiskers' expression turned serious. "I didn't hear anything. But this place... Grizzleham has its oddities."

Arthur wasn't so sure. His hand hovered just above the Golden Gravy Boat, but he couldn't shake the feeling that something— someone—was watching.

And from somewhere deep within the swirling gravy clouds above, a pair of glowing eyes glimmered.

Chapter 8
The Giant Spoon
of Gravy Justice

The Golden Gravy Boat shimmered before
Arthur, its creamy, luxurious contents rippling
like liquid treasure. Light from Grizzleham
floating gravy orbs danced across the golden
hull, making it look like the crown jewel of
condiments. Arthur took a step forward, heart
pounding.

Then, without warning, the lake rumbled.

From the churning depths, something enormous
began to rise. Arthur staggered back, wide-eyed.

It was a Giant Spoon.

It towered into the sky, easily three times the height of a dragon. Its surface gleamed like battle-hardened steel—part weapon, part kitchen utensil, all terrifying. The spoon spun once in the air, casting shimmering gravy droplets across the sky like a greasy firework, before slamming into the lake with a resounding splash that sent shockwaves through the syrup bridges of Grizzleham. The force of the impact sent Baron Twitchwhiskers flying backward, his monocle launching off his face and plopping straight into the gravy. Arthur, ever the unfortunate soul, was soaked yet again.

Only Wobblebottom remained completely unbothered, lounging in the shallows on a floating cheese log, gnawing on a gravy-covered biscuit. He watched the scene unfold with sleepy indifference, like he had seen it all before.

A booming voice echoed across the lake, so deep and resonant that even the syrup bridges seemed to tremble.

"WHO DARES disturb the sacred Golden Gravy Boat of Grizzleham?!"

Arthur, drenched from head to toe in gravy, straightened up.

"Uh... me? King Arthur of Wobblealot. And, uh, my Companions. But mostly me," he said, attempting to sound brave, though his voice wavered just a bit.

The Spoon rose higher, its enormous bowl gleaming ominously. "I am the Giant Spoon of Gravy Justice! None may claim the Golden Gravy Boat unless they prove their worth through the Trial of Gravy Combat!"

Baron Twitchwhiskers, now standing with his tail wringing out like a mop, hissed in frustration. "We don't have time for trials! There's a parade to get to!" He pointed dramatically at the Spoon. "We've got gravy to save, and a schedule to keep!"

Arthur turned to him. "Any idea how to fight... that?" He gestured toward the massive, hovering spoon, which seemed to be gleaming with malicious intent.

Baron Twitchwhiskers narrowed his eyes and adjusted his monocle, which was now thoroughly soaked in gravy. "We outmaneuver it. Confuse it. It's just a spoon, Arthur. A really big one. Every spoon has a weakness—it's called not having hands."

Arthur blinked. "Not having hands... What are we, fighting a kitchen appliance or a bad philosophy?"

"Same difference," muttered Baron Twitchwhiskers.

Arthur didn't have time to argue. He grabbed a small spoon from a floating condiment tray nearby, holding it up like a sword, though it felt more like a butter knife against a dragon's scale. "Alright then. Let's stir things up."

The Giant Spoon screeched downward with a metallic wail, sending a tidal wave of gravy crashing toward them. Arthur and Baron Twitchwhiskers barely managed to dodge, slipping and sliding through the thick mess. Wobblebottom, however, blinked lazily, barely moving as the gravy wave hit him. He casually held up his biscuit, letting it soak in the tidal wave, and took a bite. The gravy splashed over him, but it was like it didn't even exist. He was completely unfazed.

"Baron!" Arthur yelled, his voice barely audible over the roar of the gravy wave. "NOW!"

Baron Twitchwhiskers, his fur now slick with gravy, dashed across the lake, his movements surprisingly graceful for a soggy squirrel. He leapt onto a floating custard pie, using it like a sled, and crashed directly into the handle of the Giant Spoon. The spoon wobbled slightly, but it wasn't enough.

Arthur, heart pounding, saw his opening. He dashed forward; spoon raised high. In a flash of inspiration, he began performing what could only be described as interpretive stirring. He swirled the gravy in the air, sloshed it, scooped it, and jabbed it, all while shouting, "Take that, Spoon! You can't defeat the art of the swirl!"

The Giant Spoon wobbled in midair, clearly confused by this strange display of culinary combat. Baron Twitchwhiskers landed lightly on Arthur's shoulder; his fur was completely drenched. "NOW! One last swirl—make it count!"

Arthur's eyes widened with determination. He took a deep breath and, in one dramatic leap, brought his spoon down for a final, earth-shattering scoop. Gravy spiraled upward in a perfect vortex, a majestic whirlpool. The Giant Spoon flailed wildly, completely losing its balance as the gravy swirled around it, confusing its giant bowl. It spun backward, faster and faster, until it could no longer maintain control. "NOOOO!" the Spoon howled in defeat, its voice a chorus of metallic despair. "YOU HAVE OUT-STIRRED ME! I YIELD TO THE SWIRL!"

With one final, desperate wobble, the Giant Spoon crashed into the lake with a thunderous glurp, disappearing beneath the waves like a broken kitchen appliance retreating to the depths.

Arthur, soaked to the bone and exhausted, collapsed backward into the gravy. He groaned with satisfaction. "We did it," he said, his voice muffled by the gravy soaking into his clothes.

"We did it. The Spoon is... gone."

Baron Twitchwhiskers grinned widely. "You spooned up some heroics there, Arthur. I'm proud of you."

Wobblebottom, who had fallen asleep during the whole ordeal, blinked, slowly clapping while still holding a half-eaten meatball.

Arthur sighed and wiped gravy from his face. "Yeah, something. Now what?"

Baron Twitchwhiskers looked over at the now-dominating Golden Gravy Boat, which gleamed triumphantly before them. He jumped into it with glee. "Now we take it to the Royal Gravy Parade and show the world how we saved it!

Arthur smiled, the weight of the moment sinking in. "You know," he said, flopping back in the boat beside them, "I'm starting to think maybe this whole quest was a bit of a ...gravy train." With a mischievous glint in his eyes.

Wobblebottom snorted again, the sound unmistakably like laughter—or possibly the deep, rumbling echo of a particularly enthusiastic fart. Either way, it was the kind of noise only a hippo could make in such a glorious moment of triumph.

Chapter 9
Wobblebottom Saves the Day
(and Then Eats It)

The Gravy Parade had just reached its grand finale
when a sudden rumble shook the ground beneath
Arthur's feet. The Golden Gravy Boat wobbled, as if
it were about to capsize from sheer weight alone.
But it wasn't the gravy-drenched revelers or the
hippo-sized Wobblebottom rolling around in the
gravy lake that caused the disturbance.

No. It was him.

Out of the misty gravy clouds, the villain emerged.

He was tall. He was menacing. He was covered
in gravy—but not in the good way. This man
looked like he had been bathing in gravy,
straining it through his mustache. His name
was Lord Lardington, and he had come for the
Golden Gravy Boat.

"My precious... my Gravy Boat..." he growled,
his voice as thick and rich as the gravy
dripping from his chin. He reached out with
both hands, his fingers trembling like
someone who'd been deprived of the most
sacred, gravy-drenched feast. "It's mine, you
fools! I shall have it, and with it, I will flood

this pathetic kingdom with gravy! No one can stop me now!"

Arthur, who had been peacefully admiring the sunset over the gravy lake (and by "sunset," he meant the reflection of the gravy clouds), suddenly stood up and raised a hand.

"Stop right there, Lord Lardington!" Arthur shouted dramatically. "You cannot have the Golden Gravy Boat! We, the champions of Grizzleham, have won it fair and—"

HIC!

Arthur stopped mid-sentence and grabbed his throat.

HIC!

"Uh... I think I might have the hiccups," Arthur mumbled, as the entire Gravy Parade watched in confusion.
HIC!

"Look, Lord Lardington, you don't understand," Arthur continued, trying to steady himself. "We've earned this! The Golden

Gravy Boat is ours by right! You can't just waltz in and—"

HIC!

Lord Lardington sneered, dripping gravy from the tip of his mustache. "Hiccups?" he scoffed, his voice dripping with contempt. "You think hiccups can stop me? I will take this Gravy Boat, and I will use it to drown this entire kingdom in gravy! There's nothing you can do—"

But before he could finish his villainous monologue, a sound louder than a thousand pots of boiling gravy exploded from the lake.

SPLAT!

A hippo-sized blur flew out of the water, flailing in the air like a giant, slippery doughnut. It was none other than Sir Wobblebottom, hero of the kingdom, who had just bellyflopped with all his might.

The impact sent Lord Lardington flying through the air, his villainous mustache flapping wildly. He crashed into the ground with a grunt, completely submerged in gravy.

Wobblebottom landed on top of him, his enormous, round belly squashing the villain into the gravy like a giant pie. Lord Lardington's face was buried in gravy, his arms flailing helplessly.

Arthur, still struggling with his hiccups, attempted to deliver a noble speech but could only manage:

HIC! "We... we hic... we're the hic champions! We've... won the... hic... day!"

Baron Twitchwhiskers, perched on the edge of the gravy boat with a tiny cup of gravy in his paw, casually raised his cup in the air. "Well, that was one way to solve a villain problem," he said with a knowing nod.

Wobblebottom, meanwhile, was rolling around in the gravy— having completely forgotten about Lord Lardington—and instead turned his attention to something far more important: lunch.

His eyes twinkled with pure joy as he spotted a tray of crispy, gravy-covered potatoes floating by on the parade float.

With a happy snort, Wobblebottom reached out and grabbed a whole tray of fries, dipped them generously in gravy, and began to chow down. He let out a contented snort.

"I think that's it, then," Arthur said with a grin, wiping gravy off his makeshift trousers. "The Golden Gravy Boat is safe. And I suppose... lunch is saved too."

As Lord Lardington tried to claw his way out of the gravy pile (and ultimately gave up), Arthur managed a shaky salute, hiccupping once more. "So, this is how it ends, huh? With Wobblebottom bellyflopping a villain into submission, and saving the day... and then eating all the fries?"

Baron Twitchwhiskers nodded wisely, taking another sip from his gravy ladle. "Absolutely. I can't imagine a more fitting ending for this tale of adventure, sauce, and heroism."
Arthur gave one final, dramatic flourish as he stood up, hiccupping the last bit of his speech.

HIC! "To Wobblebottom... the true hero of Grizzleham, who not only saved the day but also saved lunch."

Wobblebottom snorted in approval, licking his gravy-covered lips. He leaned back, rubbing his overly stuffed stomach, when suddenly, without warning, he raised his backside and let out an almighty fart.

It was so loud, it echoed across the kingdom, vibrating the very air around them. The sheer power of it sent nearby gravy fries flying into the air. Even the clouds in the gray sky seemed to tremble in response.

Arthur, still struggling with the hiccups, blinked at the massive display of gaseous glory. "

Well.. I guess that's how we end the day, huh?"

The kingdom cheered, gravy splashing every which way as the day's festivities came to a close. The Golden Gravy Boat was safe. Lord Lardington was thoroughly defeated (mostly by sheer hippo weight). And Grizzleham gravy celebration ended with a truly glorious splash.

Arthur sighed with relief. "Well... I guess that's the end of this ridiculous quest, huh?"

Baron Twitchwhiskers, staring fondly at the gravy lake, smiled. "For now. But you never know when another villain will show up, ready to take the Golden Gravy Boat... or, you know, when Wobblebottom gets hungry again."

And with that, the Gravy Parade ended—not with a bang, but with a bellyflop, a hiccup, and a lot of very full bellies.

Epilogue: The Return of the Heroes (and Their Pants)

The sun dipped low over the Kingdom of Wobblealot, casting a warm glow across the land as Arthur and Wobblebottom sailed back into the harbor aboard the Golden Gravy Boat.

The boat, which had now officially become more of a mobile snack bar than anything else, rocked gently in the bay. The people of Wobblealot were waiting—waving, cheering, and... Well... bouncing.

Yes, bouncing. Because in Wobblealot, it wasn't a parade without a few bouncy surprises.

The streets were lined with enormous inflatable jellyfish, each one wobbling in the breeze, casting a colorful, squishy glow on the town square. The confetti that filled the air was made of tiny, soft cloud puffs, which floated lazily to the ground. Some were in the shape of tiny balloon animals, others in the form of fluttering dancing pastries—but all were spectacularly wobbly.

Arthur stood at the bow of the Golden Gravy
Boat, his crown still askew (thanks to the
curse of the dancing pants), waving with all
the grace of a confused penguin. Beside him,
Wobblebottom waddled with the air of a hippo
who had saved the day—if saving the day also
meant eating the entire town's stash of
leftover parade snacks and accidentally
flattening a few of the wobbly jelly sculptures.

The crowd erupted into cheers. They clapped.
They sang. They threw more confetti—some of
which landed perfectly on Wobblebottom,
where it got caught in his wobbly folds. The
banners that lined the streets read:
"Wobblealot's Heroes Return!" and "Long
Live the Hippo!" There was even one banner
that seemed to say, "Wobblebottom for
President of Pancakes," though Arthur wasn't
entirely sure why that was a thing.

Trumpets blared in a fanfare of triumphant
toot-toots—the kind of sound you'd hear if you
asked a band of squirrels to form a brass
section. It was cheerful, but a little off-key.
Arthur raised his hand in an attempt to look

regal, though the hiccups had returned, and this only made him seem like he was trying to win a contest for Most Awkward King.

"HIC! Thank you! Thank you, everyone! We've... we've returned victorious!" he shouted, his voice catching in the middle of the sentence. His crown slipped further, now nearly covering his eyes. He quickly straightened it with one hand, while the other awkwardly waved at the crowd.

"And let's not forget the true hero of the hour!" Arthur continued, his hiccups still making him sound like a frog caught in a windstorm. "Sir Wobblebottom.!"

The crowd cheered louder, their applause shaking the wobbly jellyfish that lined the streets. Wobblebottom, not one for speeches, let out a loud snort of approval and gave the crowd a casual belly-wobble, causing the soft puffball confetti to scatter everywhere. He promptly rolled through the confetti, absorbing it like some kind of giant wobbly sponge, and then ate a few of the cloud-pastries that had been tossed in the air.

At the back of the crowd, Kevin, the stable boy, stood frozen, eyes as wide as saucers. He wasn't exactly known for his bravery, but the sight of a giant hippo rolling through wobbly confetti, snacking on pastries, seemed to paralyze him.

Arthur hopped down from the boat with a grin. "Kevin, old friend! What have you been up to while I was off saving the kingdom from—well, let's just say strange things?"
Kevin, as always, jumped at the sound of his name. "M-MM'lord! Y-Y-Your Majesty! The jousting horse... uh... he's still gone..."

Arthur's eye twitched. "Still? For the love of jelly, Kevin—he's run off with the jousting instructor's daughter again, hasn't he?"

Kevin nodded. "Y-Yes, Your Majesty... b-but the good news is, I've... I've tried to find them! I did! But—"

Arthur sighed, rolling his eyes. "Kevin, if you're scared of the horse, it's fine. I don't expect you to go toe-to-hoof with him. Just leave it to one of the castle guards."

Kevin blinked rapidly, his face the color of a ripe tomato.

"But... but... what if he gets angry?"

"I'll deal with it," Arthur said, patting him on the shoulder with forced calm. "Just... go inside and make sure there's no more dancing pants. Please."

Kevin nodded frantically and dashed off toward the castle, moving faster than a scared rabbit.

Arthur turned back to Wobblebottom, who had already consumed most of the parade's confetti and was now happily rolling over to a large pile of fluffy cupcakes.

"Well, my trusty hippo friend," Arthur said, giving Wobblebottom's enormous belly a friendly pat, "we've made it home. Just like that."

Wobblebottom snorted and gave Arthur a side-eye, as if to say:

"Don't even think about it. These cupcakes are mine."

Just then, a royal messenger appeared, practically tripping over his excitement as he handed Arthur a scroll. "Your

Majesty! A message from the Royal Jousting School!"

Arthur, still trying to recover from the absurdity of his life, took the scroll and read aloud:

Dear King Arthur,

It is with a mix of disbelief and mild exasperation that we inform you that your horse has, once again, run off—this time, in pursuit of becoming a Champion Jousting Steed (with the help of the jousting instructor's daughter, who we suspect may have inadvertently become his "training partner" in this wild quest).

After multiple wild goose chases (and one startled goose), we've decided that the best course of action is to officially enroll your horse in the Royal Jousting School, where he will receive proper instruction in the art of jousting. No more running away. No more "accidental" stampedes. No more uninvited appearances at local festivals.

We understand that he believes the instructor's daughter is some sort of magical Jousting Genie who can make him a champion overnight, but we assure you that he will have to settle for the traditional methods—such as practice, discipline, and not galloping off at random intervals.

Your horse is now officially a student of the Royal Jousting School. We trust that you will agree that this is for his good, and we will do our best to restrain him from any further unsanctioned escapes.

 Yours (begrudgingly),

The Royal Jousting School

"We teach horses to joust. We do not chase them across the kingdom."

Arthur blinked, holding the scroll like it was an ancient artifact. "So... My horse is now a professional jouster?"

Baron Twitchwhiskers, who had appeared
out of nowhere with his tiny monocle still
crooked, scratched his chin thoughtfully.
"Well, Your Majesty, I suppose this is as close
to 'normal' as things can get here."

Arthur turned back to the jubilant crowd,
who were still clapping and cheering, and
waved awkwardly. His crown slipped to the
side, causing him to look even more
questionably regal.

"Alright, everyone!" Arthur shouted, trying to
make it sound like he had his life together.

"We've had a lot of excitement, but I think we can
all agree...

Home is where the wobble is!"

The crowd erupted into laughter and more
cheering, and Sir Wobblebottom, in a final act of
heroism, belly-flopped into a conveniently placed
pile of watermelon rinds, causing a spectacular
mess and knocking over a barrel of apples in the
process.

Arthur sighed, but couldn't help but smile. His
crown was crooked. His horse was now a
professional jouster. His best friend was a
hippo who ate everything in sight. And Kevin,
well... Kevin was still terrified of a horse.

As the final cheers died down, Kevin rushed
over to Arthur, holding something that looked
a little more regal than the tablecloth Arthur
had been wearing. It was Arthur's royal robe,
fresh and unwrinkled, with a few added
flourishes from the royal laundress, no doubt.

Arthur smiled and took the robe from Kevin,
suddenly feeling a little more like himself.

"Ah, Kevin, my loyal stable boy. You do know
how to bring a king's dignity back."

Kevin beamed, proud of himself for the first time all day. "I-I thought you might need it, Your Majesty."

Arthur slipped into the robe with a dramatic flourish. "Ahh, much better. No more tablecloths for me." He adjusted the robe and gave Kevin a wink. "Thanks, Kevin. Now, let's get back to the royal duties, shall we?"

Kevin, still a little shaken by the events of the day, nodded eagerly. "Of course, you're Majesty!"

Arthur turned to Baron Twitchwhiskers, who was eyeing a particularly large bowl of jelly in the corner. "You know, Twitchwhiskers," Arthur said, "I never did properly thank you for helping in the quest for the Golden Gravy Boat. You were a master of getting hopelessly lost, and yet somehow always finding exactly what we needed."

Baron Twitchwhiskers adjusted his tiny monocle and grinned. "It was nothing, your Majesty. Though I must say, I think my talents would be better suited in a more prestigious role... perhaps Royal Advisor?"

Arthur grinned. "I think that sounds like a fine idea. We'll get you a robe.

"And so, with that, the Parade ended—not with a bang, but with a bellyflop, a hiccup, a crown desperately clinging to Arthur's head like a drunken squirrel, and a whole lot of very full, very happy bellies. But just as the crowd began to settle, Sir Wobblebottom, in all his glory, raised his backside to the sky and let out a glorious, thunderous fart that shook the very earth beneath them. It was the perfect punctuation to a perfectly absurd day."

Thank you